Sometimes SNOW Falls in the SUMMER

Story and Illustrations by deb troehler

For Gregory, my best friend, my H.B.

Thank you to Liz Violett, Marilyn Parker, and Berdine Creedy
for your contributions to this book.

"Do you think they'll fit?" asked Ella, staring wide-eyed at the huge pile of clothes on her bed.

Momma squeezed a pair of shorts into the suitcase and replied, "I think so." She then opened the closet door and pulled out a pair of well-worn sneakers. "These are perfect!"

"Eww! They're dirty. Why do I have to take those ole' things?" complained Ella.

"Ella, they're just the thing for your treks around Nana's pond, especially when the snow starts to fly," said Momma.

Ella had forgotten about the summer snows. "Tell me again how it snows in the summer? Please. Is it really that cold?"

Momma laughed. "Sweetie. It doesn't have to be cold for it to snow at your Nana's farm. With a bit of patience, you'll see."

Patience—that word again. Momma was always telling Ella she had to be more patient. Yet, to a seven-year-old who lived in the big city, patience was usually in short supply.

"Oh, I'm sure you'll find your patience on your trip to Nana's farm," said Momma.

While Momma finished her packing, Ella thought about the stories that she'd heard so often. Momma's childhood home in Northern Michigan had been filled with magic.

Nana could turn thread as thin as a spider's web into beautiful clothing fit for a princess.

On breezy summer days, Nana's magic filled Momma's bedroom with rainbows that danced on the ceiling.

Sometimes snow even fell in the summer! Life in the country was definitely special.

Ella was curious. "Momma, if you had so much fun on Nana's farm, why'd you move to the city?" she asked.

"Honey, your daddy and I moved here to be close to his work. Besides, magic can be found anywhere. You simply need to take the time to look." Momma wiggled the sneakers into the suitcase. "There. That should do it. We have just enough time to make it to the airport."

Ella took one last look at her bedroom. Seven days seemed oh-so-very-long. Although she loved her grandmother dearly, Ella had never been to her home in the country. Momma smiled and gave her daughter a reassuring hug. "Ella Louise, I just know you'll have a terrific time with Nana. She makes everyday life so much fun."

Ella took a deep breath and said, "I guess I'm ready to go."

Departures

Flight 316

Status: Boardi

Traverse City,

At the airport, Momma pinned a special tag onto Ella's shirt. "Honey, please do exactly what the flight attendant says. Nana will meet you as soon as you get off the plane." She gave her daughter a big hug. "I'll miss you, Sweetie."

The flight attendant smiled at Ella and took her hand. "Ella, we're going to have lots of fun on the plane. I'll make sure you have a seat by the window. 'Ready to go?"

Ella forced a smile. Then she and the attendant disappeared into the corridor that led to the plane.

The plane soon left the airport. Ella watched her big town on

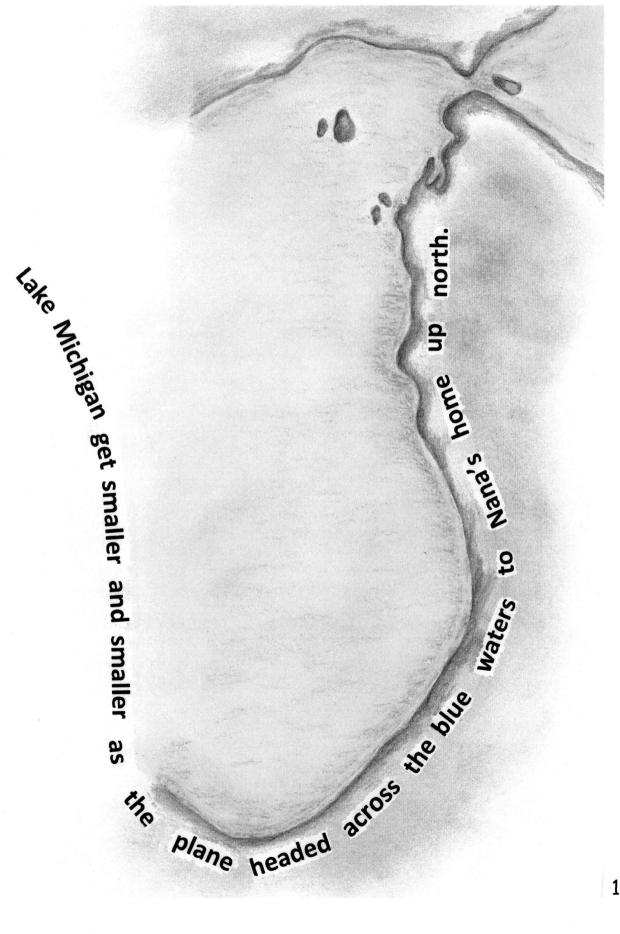

Lake Michigan get smaller and smaller as the plane headed across the blue waters to Nana's home up north.

Arrivals
Flight 316
Status: On Tim
Chicago, IL

When the plane landed, Ella cautiously stepped through the door. She was a bit scared, but her fears quickly faded when she saw the smiling face of her grandmother. "Nana!" she called, running to give her a hug. Nana picked up Ella's suitcase and the two of them embarked on their adventure.

The rain had stopped by the time they reached Nana's home. At first, Ella was a bit disappointed. The house was quite plain. How did Momma ever think this place was so magical?

When they got out of the car, a silver tabby came running from beneath the porch to greet them. "Ah, Miss Tiggles. You've come to greet our visitor," said Nana.

"She's pretty," said Ella, reaching down to pet the cat." And friendly, too. I wish we could have a kitty at home, but Daddy says they aren't allowed in our building."

Ella gave the cat a pat on the head and scurried into the farmhouse.

"I don't see them! I thought rain brought the rainbows."

Nana closed the front door and chuckled, "Oh, there will be rainbows. In this house we don't need the rain to make them appear. With a little patience, you'll see."

Ella groaned. "Here, too?"

Ella and Nana spent the rest of the evening sorting through Nana's big basket of yarn. Miss Tiggles played at their feet while Ella picked her colors. "Sweetie, by the time you leave, this yarn will be a pretty sweater for the chilly summer nights at home."

Lost in thought, Ella dangled a piece of yarn and watched as Miss Tiggles jumped up to grab it. "A cat is the perfect pet. I wish we could have one."

"Sweetie, you can have a cat to take back home with you. We just need to be sure it's the right kind of cat. Let's see." Nana went to the corner of the room and picked up an old hatbox that was overflowing with scraps of fabric. "Hmm. Would you like a pink cat or a green cat? How about one with stripes?"

Suddenly Ella understood. "Pink. I think my cat should be pink." Together they looked through the fabric until they had just enough to make a stuffed cat.

That night Ella went to sleep dreaming of the kitty she was going to make.

The next morning, Ella was awakened by the gentle purring of Miss Tiggles. When she reached out to pet her she noticed the cat's keen eyes were intently staring at something on the ceiling. Ella looked up.

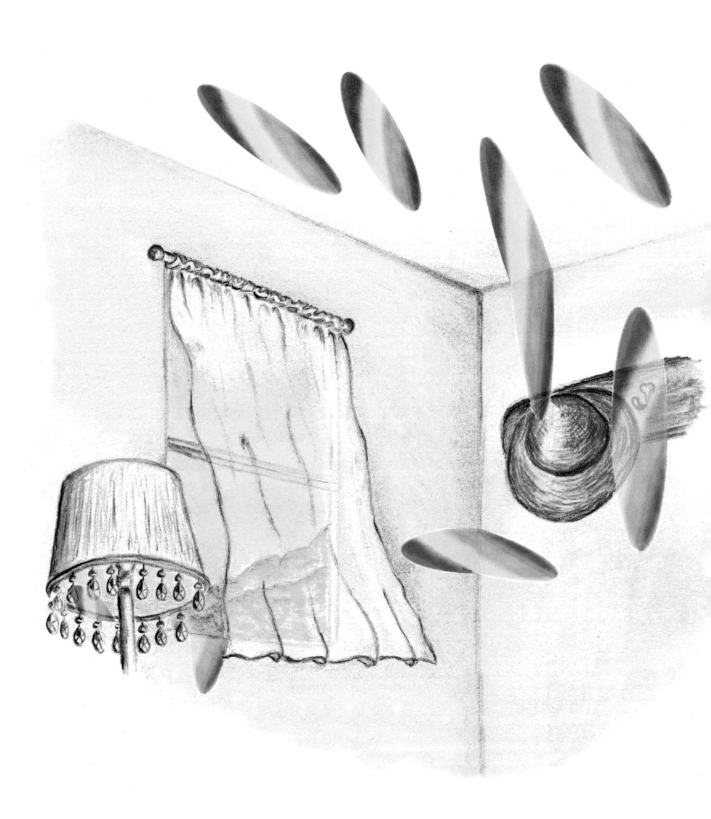

"The rainbows! Those are the rainbows Momma told me about!"

The clouds had cleared, and bright rays of sunshine streamed into her window. Prisms dangling from the bedside lamp had captured the rays, sending splashes of color everywhere.

Hearing Ella's excitement, Nana came into her room. "Aren't they beautiful? Your momma never tired of waking to them."

Miss Tiggles batted at the prisms. "It looks like Miss Tiggles feels the same," laughed Ella.

"Well," Nana sighed, "Let's go downstairs for a big country breakfast. That will give you the energy to work on your own cat."

After breakfast they headed into the living room. Nana drew a big picture of a cat on a piece of newsprint and helped her granddaughter cut out two pieces of pink fabric. With a bit more guidance, Ella began her long task of stitching the two pieces together. Nana worked on the sweater while Ella brought her kitty to life.

As the number of stitches on the cat grew, so did the rows of blue yarn. Sometimes Ella's stitches went up when they should have gone down, but she was making progress.

By the time the stitches had reached her kitty's ears, Nana had finished the back of the sweater.

When the stitches reached the first paw, Nana had finished the front.

Eventually the two of them finished.

"Look, Nana! I'm done. Well, except for the stuffing." She thought for a moment. "What will we stuff it with?"

With a twinkle in her eye, Nana replied, "With *cattails*, of course!"

Ella didn't understand. The cattails she had seen by Nana's pond weren't fluffy at all. How could they ever be used to stuff her cat? Nevertheless, the time Ella had spent on Nana's farm had taught her that through Nana's magic, cattails would somehow become the perfect stuffing.

"Tell you what. We'll stuff your cat tomorrow, after the morning dew is gone."

The next morning Ella pulled the sneakers Momma had packed out of a plastic bag. "I'm glad Momma packed these ole' sneakers," she said as she trotted outside to join her grandmother.

The final droplets of the morning mist hovered above the water as Ella and Nana made their way to the cattails lining the banks of the pond. They gathered the tall stalks and laid them in the sun to dry while they finished their morning chores.

By mid-afternoon the cattails were dry. Nana and Ella sat down on the blanket to begin their task.

"Ella, snap off just the tip," said Nana, guiding Ella's hand. "It will happen pretty quickly after that."

When Ella snapped off the top of the stalk a big pile of fluff exploded onto the blanket.

"Wow!" she exclaimed as she ran her fingers through the quickly building mound of cattail seeds. Ella continued pulling the fluff from the stalks until there was a huge pile.

Then Nana showed her how to fill her cat by stuffing bits of the fluff into an opening in the back. "It's going to be the softest kitty around." said Ella.

They had barely finished when...

a gust of wind picked up the remaining fluff, sending it into the air in enormous swirls.

Ella squealed with delight, "Momma was right!" she shouted. "It *does* snow in the summer!"

As Nana stitched the final seam on Ella's cat, she paused for a moment and gazed at her granddaughter dancing on the grass, arms stretched wide, surrounded by a blizzard of cattail fluff.

HOW MUCH SNOW DOES IT TAKE TO FILL A SAND PAIL?

MESSY FUN: This activity is intended to be completed outside. Please see alternate activity on the next page.

MATERIALS NEEDED:

Cattails that have been dried
Weights and Balance
Two identical bowls or two sand pails

WORDS TO KNOW: weight, mass, density, volume

INSTRUCTIONS:

1. Parents: prior to the activity prepare two bowls—one with a cattail that is intact and one with a cattail that has had the seeds removed and placed into the bowl with the stalk.
2. Let's compare the contents of the two bowls. Which one do you think has more mass (stuff)?
3. Use the balance and weights to determine the density of each. How could one bowl have more space filled and still have the same mass?
4. Select a cattail the approximate size of the one used in step 1.
5. Use the weights and balance to determine the mass of the cattail and bowl.
6. Carefully pull the seeds (the brown-coated fluff) off of the cattail and place into the empty bowl. Remember to place the stalk into the bowl.
7. Use the weights and balance to determine the mass of the bowl and cattail fluff. Why does the bowl of fluff have the same mass?

ANSWER:
When the cattail seeds are on the stalk, they are packed tightly together. There is not much air between the seeds. When the seeds are pulled off of the stalk, air is combined with the seeds, causing them to take up more room in the bowl. The mass is the same, but the density is different. The intact cattail has higher density because the seeds are closer together.

FOLLOW-UP FUN: After completing the activity, see who can blow their summer snow (cattail seeds) the furthest by fanning a clump of the seeds with a piece of paper or book.

FUN FACT: Cattails have also been called corn dog grass and bulrush. Conduct an internet search to find the origin of those names. Which name do you like best?

HOW FAR CAN YOU THROW A PAPER SNOWBALL?

CLEAN FUN: This activity is an alternative to the messier activity on the previous page.

MATERIALS NEEDED:

30-40 sheets of white 20 lb. printer paper
Two identical bowls or sand pails
Ruler or tape measure

WORDS TO KNOW: air friction, resistance

INSTRUCTIONS:

1. Parents: at the beginning of the activity have the children try to toss a flat piece of paper as far as they can. Why do you think it is difficult to toss the paper? How could we make it easier to toss?
2. Lightly crumple another piece of paper into a ball. (a paper snowball) Measure how wide the ball is.
3. Throw the flat paper and the crumpled paper. Which is easier to toss? Why?
4. Crumple another piece of paper into a tighter paper ball. Measure how wide the ball is.
5. Take turns throwing both balls of paper to see which one can be thrown the furthest. Why does one ball travel farther than the other one?
6. Which sized snowball would be better to make to use for a snowball toss race? Why?

ANSWER:
When the flat paper is tossed, it meets with resistance as it is tossed into the air. There is more surface slowing it down. When the paper is crumpled, the surface area is reduced, which reduces the way it is slowed in the air. The tightly crumpled paper also has a smaller surface area than the loosely crumpled paper; therefore the air doesn't slow it down as much.

FOLLOW-UP FUN: Crumple paper into balls to fill the bowls or sand pails. Divide into teams and take turns seeing who can throw the snowballs the furthest distance. Measure the distance.

FROSTY FUN: Conduct an internet search to find the last recorded date for snowfall in your town.

For questions, please contact me at dtroehler@aol.com

Made in the USA
Columbia, SC
28 December 2022

75145843R00022